THE NEVER WAS

TYLER KNOTT GREGSON

2025

Painting used on the cover is by James Abbott McNeill Whistler, Nocturne in Black and Gold, the Falling Rocket, 1875, oil on panel. Detroit Institute of Arts, Gift of Dexter M. Ferry, Jr., 46.309.

Published by Central Avenue Poetry, an imprint of Central Avenue Marketing Ltd.
centralavenuepublishing.com

THE NEVER WAS

Trade Paper: 978-1-77168-421-7
Ebook: 978-1-77168-422-4

Printed in United States of America

1. POETRY / Subjects & Themes - American 2. POETRY / Love

1 3 5 7 9 10 8 6 4 2

SLY

Half a life
breathless,
as many
take our breath
away,
so few, I'm learning,
finally give it
back.

Never will I not
weep or sob, slow tears
or quiet gasp in the center
where breath should live
but cannot anymore,
never will I not
when seeing that thin ribbon
insulating us
from all that black.

We round dwellers sharing
space with morphos blue
and birds that hum,
with all that howls
in canopy or treeline,
just beyond the shore
of lake.

Fragile,
this illuminated place,
and we forget
as a million creatures
will be no more,

that it was not made
for us.

Autism
the alien ship
of me
deep in an empty part
of space,

the rare orbit
close enough to
earth
to pick up signals

before vanishing
back
into the black
once more.

I am isolation
decorated with fierce
curiosity.

9155

DO NOT MAIL

INTER-DEPARTMENTAL
CORRESPONDENCE

Ink-covered hands,
arms,
fingertips
and clothes.

I am filthy
with the stories
I have been
trying
to tell.

CONFIDENTIAL

Wish that when death rang
my number (a number it knew
by heart)
I'd go like

whale fall,

silent to the darkest part
of the coldest
sea

and once home
on the bottom, once
still,

feed a thousand
thousand things
that no one will ever
see.

In the hilarity of happenstance,
the serendipity
of a single second,
our lives are formed.

What of words we did not speak,
roads we never
walked down? What of
wishes abandoned
before the granting,
what of the half moment
we waited before stepping
out of the house?

Everything I have,
born from some ridiculous
twist of fate.
There are ten billion men
I could have been,

ten billion more
I could be.

If it wasn't for
drifting
away,
we'd never end
where
we were
always supposed
to
end.

Some knots
are meant to
come
untied.

I'm not here, not always, I'm a helium balloon
with a poorly tied knot.
I'm up and off and away and you
are smaller by the moment. Humans
aren't great jumpers, not built that way,
and so I'm off and lost in some patch
of sky and wobbling on the edge of
fear and excitement and I know
I don't know where I'm gonna end up.

This is the mind of the man before you,
bag of snakes I lost count of,
coiled,and I cannot remember which
are venomous. In the middle
of some moment I'm heartbroken
about lonely letters in an alphabet,
I'm picnic table plans and part lists
because I saw a photograph
of some Danish shoreline
and a perfect place to eat lunch.

I heard an idea once that when two men meet,
there are six men present: each man as he sees himself,
each as seen by each, and each as he truly is. I shook for
an hour after reading this, wondering what it means
that if I meet a man, I don't see myself, and I am what I
am, only.
Maybe some are one thing, unchanging
despite a world that wants to mold you,
maybe I am this, maybe it's the best thing
or the worst thing about me.

Dare I name myself,
speak out artist, shout out
poet, painter, lover,
or romantic?
Am I worthy of the label,
is it worthy of me?
These are umbrellas,
and I think I fear their
shade,
these are shadows
and wouldn't I miss the
sun?

Am I warrior, peacemaker,
Buddhist or Brave? Could I
call myself boring, genius,
or lunatic, three breaths from
straight-jacket and padded
walls?

I am nothing,
though I create more
than I destroy. I call myself
nothing, as it stays unshared.
Easy from the mouth rolls
this, nothing, says teeth
to tongue.

I am many things,
though I hover between them,
equator between poles,
craving for sweetness untasted.
I am bardo.

I am everything,
I am all things simultaneously,
the umbrella and the rain,
the shadow and the light
splintering off, warming
every single thing
it touches.

The ravens, too,
caught their voices
and called them back,
silent,

and turned to face
the last shards
of light

stab through the
clouds
holding tight
on the horizon
line.

I am the unhinged expression
of affection unrestrained,

I am the wilder shows
of love,
the unfolded arms
from straight-jacket
madness,

outstretched and shaking,

the mania before the
stillness when you
fall into

them.

I'm to be built on new stuff,
or the old that sleeps in the
darker corners of this soul,
the stuff I left and assumed
would grow on its own,
unwatered, away from
the light.

I'm to be gentle and curious,
patient despite reasons
to be hasty, I'm to be calm
in the face of panic.
I'm to be kindness, a wave
of compassion that consumes
and soaks all in its path.
I'm to taste of tenderness,
to make this life a poem
written in footsteps and hands
held out for the holding,
I'm to be new, or unearth
the old like excavation and
hold it to the sun as dust
falls from it like incense smoke
and discovery.

Look close, spin it in your
dirty fingers, it is I, new
though ancient.
Call me relic and wonder of
my origins, call me artifact
and wipe the residue of past
from all that used to
shine.

Soft lines like sea floor
like fossil stories told in stone

here the tale of growth,
belly big enough to hold
the planet you now call daughter,
you now call son.

Here, parable of survival
whispered in skin long since
scarred.

Put your hands to your hips
like brand new feet on
brand new sands,

show me where you grew,
show me where you
healed.

Were I to try

put paint to it,
it'd end up pitch
and tar,
night from brush
and the glitter gold
splattered
messy around the
edges.

Is darkness
a color?

This is the middle
of me,
it'd say, this
is what you'd find
if you split me
in two.

This dance the last
(until we spin again,
new)
the final flight
(with these tired
wings)
the locomotive overdue
(up the mountainside,
the steam
pouring like dragon
breath)
the swan song
(sang on dark pond,
softly)
the coda
(and what a story
we wrote)
.

And from the center
of me,
infinite strings
and knots
where they connect
to all things

and from you
and you
and they the same.

We are the web
overlapping,
all of us
the center the silk
radiates
from.

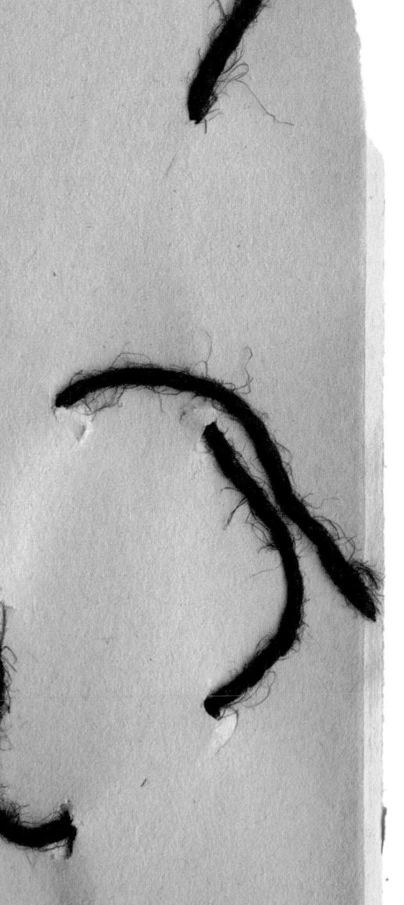

Mind like a spiral
staircase,
circles on
circles
on endless loops.

I swear one day
I'll reach the
rooftop
of this place,

one day
I'll set down
the luggage
and breathe.

One day I'll see
the city
lights.

Hand on the surface
of still waters,
falling water
off the surface
of trembling
hands.

Some of me stays
everywhere
I have been.

I am this river
I am this sea.

1956

1955

AIR POST STAMPS

ITALY

If I was nothing
or hardly much
more
would I still be
everything
and barely any
less?

Where's the line,
show me
so I remember
to
erase it.

In the pursuit of something
real,
we did what we did
and did
before that.

We leave footprints
as fossils
and marvel

when we come around again
and find that our
feet

fit so
perfectly.

In the mourning
of all that
isn't

we neglect
all that
is.

See what remains
and give it

you.

There is no
now.

We're milliseconds,
80 of them,
in the past, always
about a blink
behind.

Do what you wish,
for all else
is already
done.

A hole in a wall,
a fire to
fill it.

We'll write our
names
in the soot that
sticks,

tell our story
in ash in fingerprints

that we were here
once,
that we filled this
place

with
heat.

Andean geese
throw themselves from
clifftops,
feathers pinned to smooth sides,
dive
to certain death
when that which they chose
to love
breathes no more.

Love
is a flight-graced
creature
that silently refuses
to save itself,

to flap its own
wings.

350

Hot white light
to the
criminal
you're calling
me,

interrogated
for a mind that works
different

drowned out
in the ignorance
you can just hear me,
just make out

that different
is not
wrong.

To define an undefinable,
to wrap it up in words,
they ask what beauty is
and I stumble over myself.
A red window on a wall
of white, I think, but this
feels pedestrian and
too slim. To fight
for love, no matter the cost,
perhaps, but this
feels cliche and
too obtuse.

That which is
without asking to be,
I decide,
that which gives
without having enough
to keep.

I will not speak It,
I've no authority to decide
such matters.

THE

Were I rainfall
would it downpour
I'd be,
were I afternoon
storm,
lightning would I
bring?

Call I the agitation
of the
atmosphere,
call I fracas
of weather,

call I dark clouds
to finally
dim the
sky.

and it whispers to itself
just below the surface,
just beneath
the soil.

grow tall,
says it to it,
wide if you may,

it speaks in quaking
and rustle,
kindness to its roots,
hope to all that catches
sun

sometimes the wind
carries its voice
and we wonder at what
it says

strange what comes
when we are kind
to ourselves,

trembling giant,
biggest creature on this earth,

one thing

singing to
itself.

Call a single line
on canvas

art

if it's made of
ache
and a hand that
trembled
at its drawing

who
are we to say

otherwise?

Speak in verse fill books with words,
rise early to warm your mug,
bury the noises in mass graves
beneath ribcage, behind heartbeat,
mask them with wink and passion,
you then you then you before me

it is not enough.

Paint you in poetry, watercolor without rhyme,
go where you go when going
cuts anchor and sends it into
the dark waters in me,

hold the earth with bloody fingers,
wrap arm around root to call it balance,
stare across the fulcrum as all
stare back and fight the will to just
let go

it is not enough.

Grain of sand at
arm's length
they say, one atom
in a black sea
uncountable

each dot, each
speck of shine

a galaxy

when we know
we are
small,

what is left but
to make our
tiny lives

colossal?

Trembled once,
huddled and braced, stone walls
weeping with midnight moisture,

wrath of gods, said we,
infants with infant fears,
children on the timeline of things.

Fury, we called it, punishment
for our mortal failings, lightning
like arrows thrown earthward,

thunder like roar, like hammers
on anvils, shaping bolts
to illuminate the awe in our faces.

Air is an insulator, we learn,
barrier between charges, positive
and negative, and one day

the differences between the two
build to a breaking (as all things must
break) and must release.

Still we tremble,
backs to walls of wood, away
from the windows we stare through.

Still the fear, toddlers with
toddler fright, but now we know,
understand the math of it.

Science has come
not to steal our wonder,
but to give it back.

Won't call it wasted, not
sacrificed nor frittered away,
won't dub it worthless
nor the consequence
of miscalculation.

These were years
that answered the questions
those before have asked.

I am made for there,

I have outgrown
the man I once
was.

I of hoof and pupil square,
woolen, night shaded
in hue we once called
nothingness.

Was and am
and will be.

Man in middle,
I of crust chopped
and left for bin.

I of never in,
of out on edges,
of wallflower
skin.

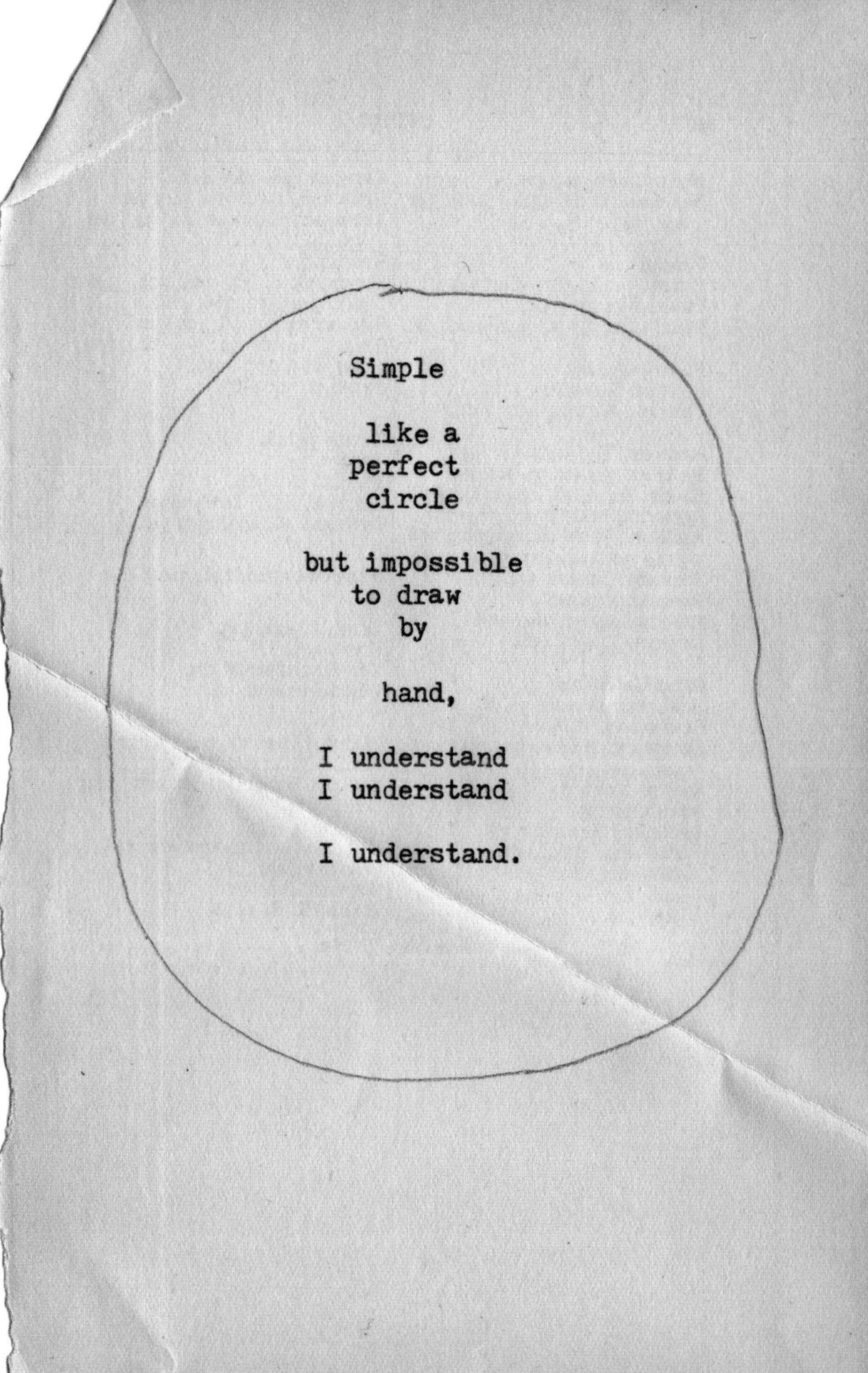

Simple

like a
perfect
circle

but impossible
to draw
by

hand,

I understand
I understand

I understand.

I'm living out lives in my dreams,
and I think they are real people.
I've no proof to offer, cannot be sure,
but I wake with their memories
and a pillow wet with the salt
from their tears.

What if then I knew what now I do,
spoke in tongues of these nocturnal few?

Here there be monsters
made in midnight hours, this
becomes that then dissolves
into what hides where moonlight
can't spill.

I am knuckles white and muscles
in my jaw overdeveloped,
as I see what they
have seen.

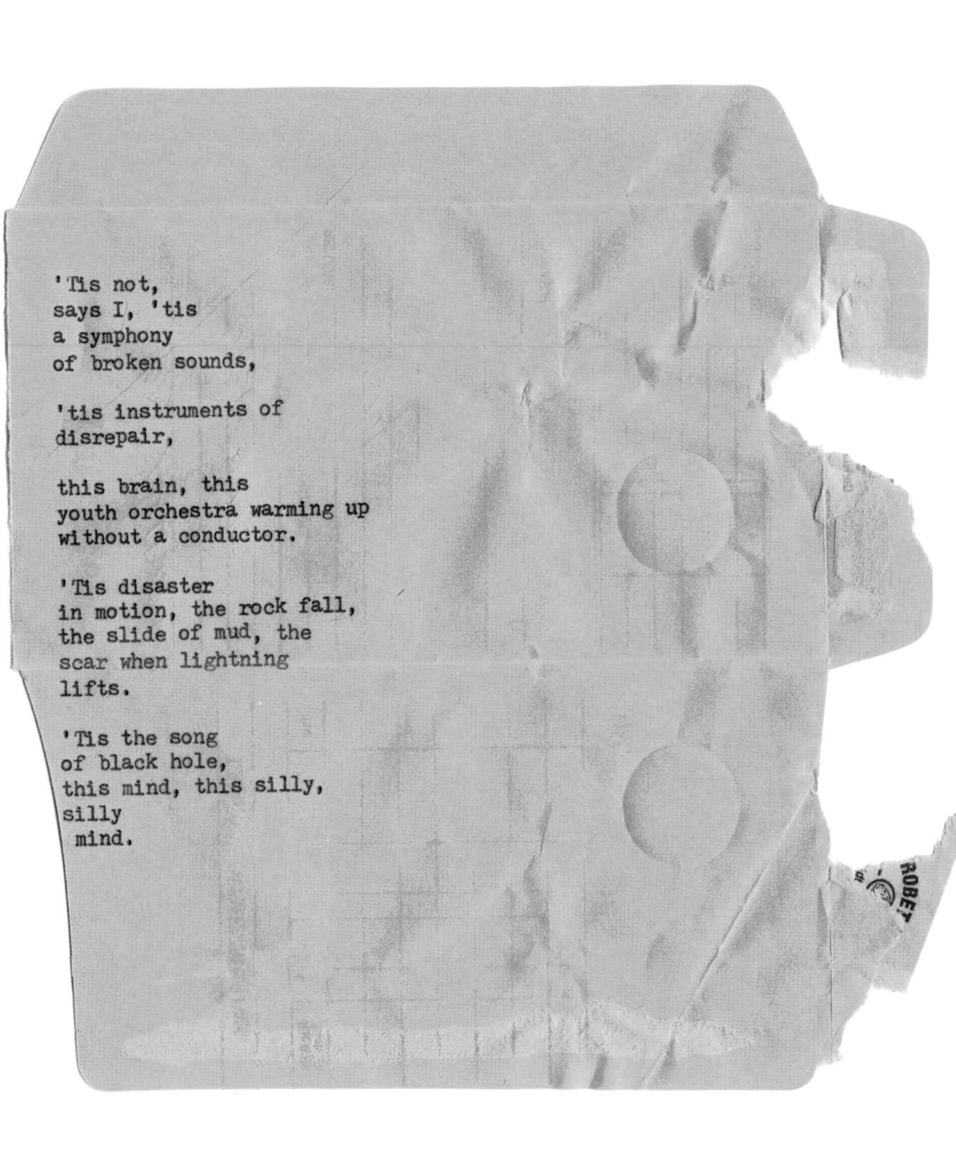

'Tis not,
says I, 'tis
a symphony
of broken sounds,

'tis instruments of
disrepair,

this brain, this
youth orchestra warming up
without a conductor.

'Tis disaster
in motion, the rock fall,
the slide of mud, the
scar when lightning
lifts.

'Tis the song
of black hole,
this mind, this silly,
silly
mind.

Bring who you were
to where you're
going
and you'll end up
staying
exactly where you
are.

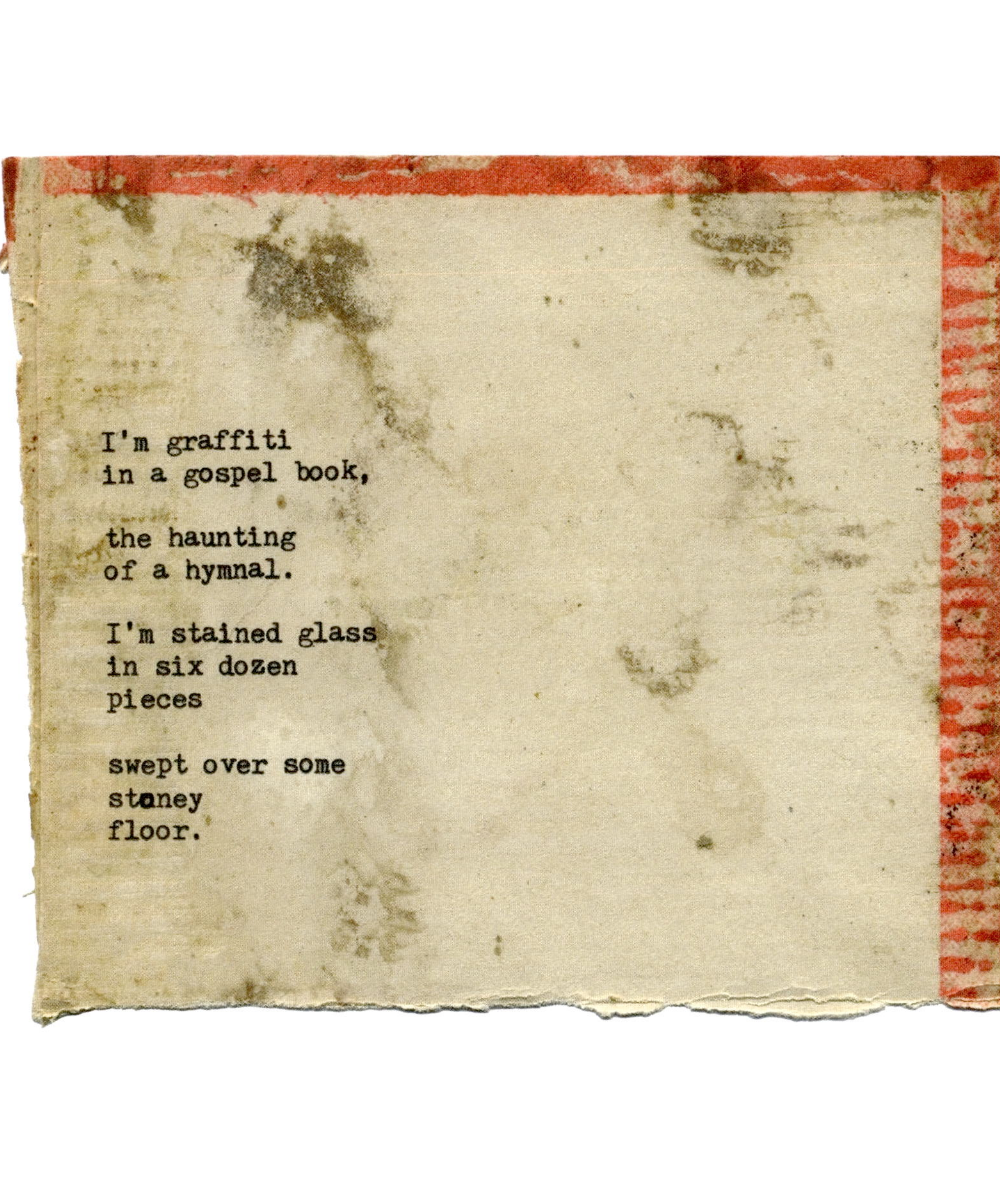

I'm graffiti
in a gospel book,

the haunting
of a hymnal.

I'm stained glass
in six dozen
pieces

swept over some
staney
floor.

In me hiding,
many,
strangers some, men
and women and those
that carry no names.

My mouth moves
when they speak, sharing lips,

some stand in line
and wait for their turn
to whisper.

I look in mirrors
away from the eyes,
they're there sometimes,
peeking back,
and it frightens me.

I look in mirrors
and call this frivolity
superfluous.

On ocean black
and ship half
sunk,

through the rigging
of my soul

I see
stars.

I of many forms, a thousand times
around this circle,
I of beard snow white and curled,
old man in doorway
handing out to the strays,
time enough for all to eat.
I of winged grace,
feathers splayed and stretching,
hawk or eagle, owl perhaps,
as birds do not bother
with what they are named.

I of sea skin, blistered
when I surface, when breath
is sought and I linger too long,
I of wide eyes and forlorn song,
eerie in the darkness when I
sing. I of hunted flesh,
seeker of a depth where
I cannot be harmed.

I of water and nothing more,
heavy in swollen cloud,
grey only to those with
upward stares, I of single
shape, elongated in the plunge
back to the dry earth,
I of teardrop from the cheek
of a thousand gods.

I of so many forms, called
five thousand names, born
and born again, trying my best
to get it right.
In the great push towards nothing,
I collect mistakes,
one more than required
to keep me returning,
just enough to tip those scales
and call me back
again.

Some let go gently,
a delicate set down
of this sweltering season,

some

slam it down
and kick it
away.

My feet sing
at the silencing
of this
heat.

I sit, heavy enough with words that standing
no longer serves. There is not sense
to be made of the spill internal,
these are those of shredded sort. I cannot
find the seams or where they match.

"The planet breathes,
its lungs are just bigger,"
rises like the unstirred starchy white water
of salted noodles that found boil,
"I am driven by shadowed hands,"
left on the dark side of some
quiet road inside.

Then you of your newfound silver
and some whisper that repeats,
then echoes over itself,
speaks of grace, of grace,
of grace,
and I rise again, and show gravity
this lightness.

You find your way
into them all,
glue to the scraps
in me.

Summer afternoon,
a heat that chokes and
steals the bumble
from the
bee.

Spoon of sugar water
and five minutes
of tenderness,

she flew
away.

You of severed
wing
flight feathers
plucked
you of gold heart
shining
through the ash

you the
reverse
staring back
you of mirror
of puddle
of window pane when
I walk
by.

You of grandeur
of such special standing,
you of
excess

one day you
too

will be a headstone

swallowed

by a tree.

I will dig
for the man
buried
beneath
the sediment
of exhaustion and
cynicism,

just below
the noise that
stirred
the avalanche.

It's guilt sometimes, an overwhelming
crush as if sky and earth conspire
to meet in the center of me.
I should love it here, I should walk
with awe-filled eyes and breathe
the dry dust like ritual smoke, should
call these trees guardians and feel
thankful for their age, rings on rings
as they stab heavenward.

There are seasons of discontent,
but I don't know the name
when seasons become years
and those spill into decades
like dam split; sometimes leaking
becomes pouring, and on to
flooding as though sublimation,
a skipping of the steps between.

I walk the same trails and breathe
the same stale and smoke-soaked air
and dream of far-off places,
I close doors behind me and fight
gravity to keep my head high,
to keep myself from shame
at the forgetting, at the amnesia
of what home once
meant.

Still
even after
perhaps because
or despite
but still
after all this
still

tempted

by the one
I have

still
by the one
that has
me

I've no dream larger,
no wish
of higher order
than this --

to become nothing
but a set of eyes
staring out
at some gloomy
ocean,

to rise like sea foam
and morning
mist

above all this
aching.

Don't touch me

Remove me please
from society,
pull the rip cord
and let me hover above it.
I've lost my taste
for the view from
the ground,
lost my patience for
the pace of this place.

Give me a life I don't need
escaping from,
give me a home
I'll never want
to leave.

Strong west winds
point me somewhere
new.

Where are the circles
to the gods of our
time,
where are the stones
that sit and catch
solstice light?

Where are the words
we will pass down,

where are the stories
that will

stay?

We are temporary
and only worship

ourselves

what will remain

when we are
gone?

Come as bones if you've nothing else,
come and speak as we once spoke,
hide the money while I shut my eyes,
while I listen to the tick tick tick
of the watch you wore to war.

Bearer of your name, I whisper
to the membrane between my home
and yours, ask the veil to lift
and count down the hours to
the autumn night I call it possible,
come and spin stories like silk
in my imagination,

tell me railroad tales, tell me
of the friends you lost, bombs louder
than the voice of god.

Come, and tell me all this
will one day make
sense.

If I gave it all
to you,
the light
harvested
over all those years
of dark,
would I
become darkness
too?

I am sorry
for the shadow
in me,

I kept no
shine

at all.

To my father

It's not brave, what I do,
though some call it that,
it's not courage
if you're not afraid.

I write to heal, to sew
up open wounds,
they tear when I wake.
Stitches that rip when
I think I hurt you
and don't know what
I said that caused
the pain. I write
to explain what I don't
have voice to,
to apologize to myself
for hating the noise
I can't seem to quiet.

Maybe this isn't poetry
but therapy, but diary
spilled out with line break
and syntax, maybe
it's all rubbish bin
quality and I'm riding
one giant wave
of luck and circumstance.

It's not brave, what I do,
it's finding my way
out of a forest I never
intended on ending up in.
It's not courage
if you're just trying to
survive.

Half chance at light
a burst through
the clouds

a reprieve
from a decade
of winter
I
am

so tired
of shivering.

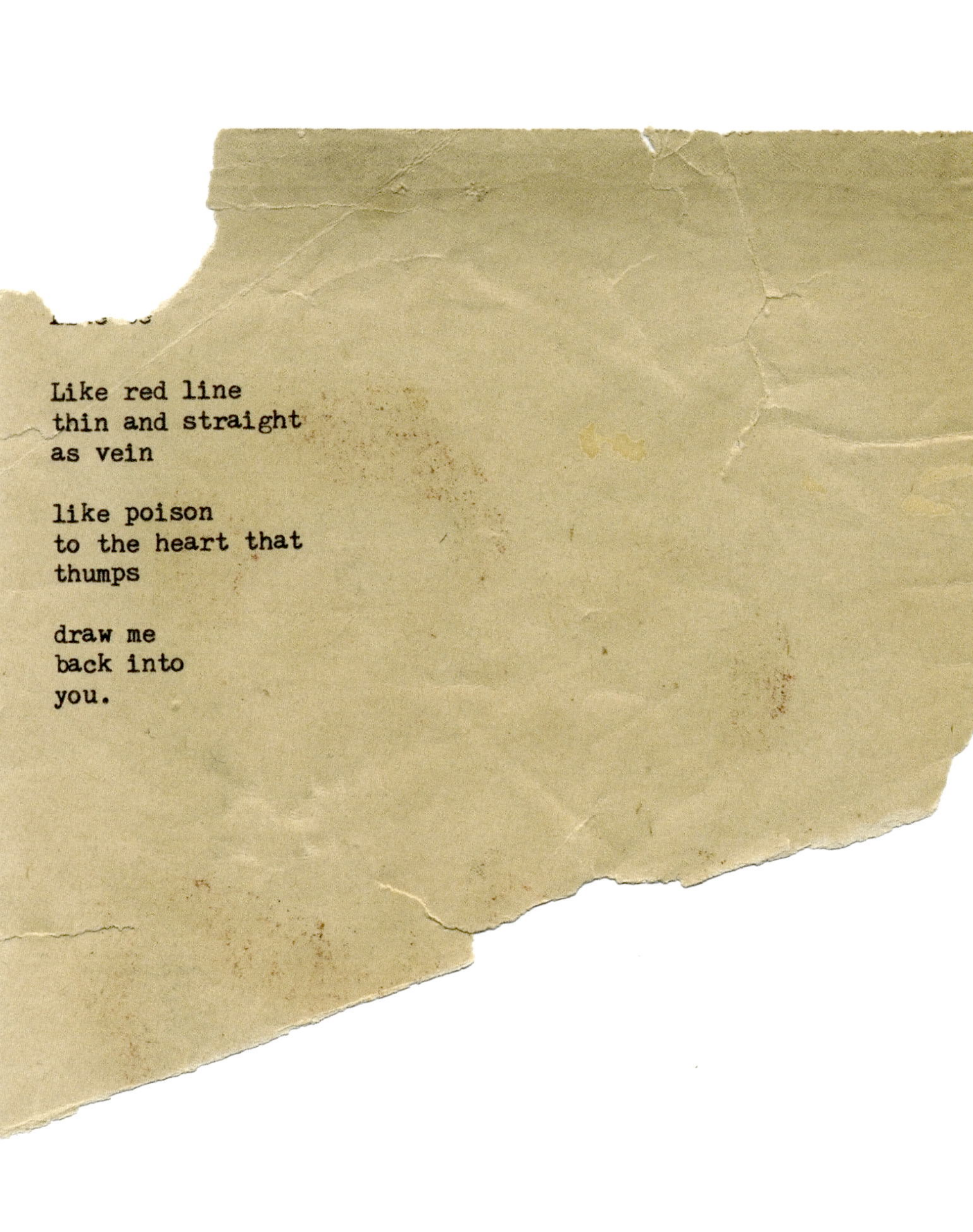

Like red line
thin and straight
as vein

like poison
to the heart that
thumps

draw me
back into
you.

I think of the empty booths
the corners I'd hide in,
think of the silence
after the din of fork on plate
after the ice melts
and soggies the napkin
below.

I think of the quiet drives
the music off
the hum of tire on road
how everywhere would become
nowhere, how I would not go
to go, but to leave it all
behind.

I think of the cold sheets,
the black hole on your side
of the bed,
the emptiness when I reach,
still half submerged
in the water of my dreams,
the gasping panic
as I drown in them,
the hand not there to pull me
back.

Please, I beg into the thoughts
thundering like typhoon in the sea
of me, please, and hope you will hear

do not go
before I
go.

If I ask
gentle enough
or scream
with just enough
ferocity

can I have all
that wonder

back?

I will not waste it
again.

Raised by the cold, by snowfalls
that come before leaves have gone,
the sound a house makes when
straining to hold its heat.

We all shudder against the freeze,
don't we?
All wrap ourselves around ourselves,
but arms grow tired
when the cold will not go.

Comes earlier and lingers longer now,
consequences of a broken place,
blue these hands, two of billions
that have done the breaking,
and brings sadness
with its frost.

It too stays longer each year,
coils like vines, like ice serpent
around the middle of me.

Sorrow does not speak
the languages I speak,
my lips too cold
for the screaming.

I am so weary
of winters.

It is an
opening
to decimation,

slow cut down
soft spread of rib,

heartbeats sound softer
without a cage
for echo.

What is love
but a ferocious risk,
a defiant willingness

to be hurt
by another?

There is
poetry
in looking
across a room,
finding eyes
looking
back
and silently
understanding
the ache
in them.

North now, corner of a border
then further still, out to the treeless,
to the barren and fog-soaked.
Returned, we, as though circle born,
beringed now, like green of Kerry,
black stone and buttercup of Beara.
Ringed on fingers, two,
hands to glass, staring into
bookshops where sorrowful poems
were pecked out onto typewriters,
half-broken as display.

She curls into me, closer like mist,
like shoreline the sea has kissed.

East now, across lonely middle,
pause at farmland, drystack
walls holding the hooved
and woolen.

Fresh now, as though made new,
soft as lamb still hiding underfoot,
unsteady steps across nettle,
bramble, and fern.

West now, to home,
carrying only what we carried,
and the gentle perfume

of warm peat smoke
from the quiet fires
they stoke.

If shutters stay open,
exposures left long,
this face would be blur,
motion trail and half a man.
Each image of us, we two,
stoic and left to our posing,

you, clear and straight glancing,

me, the profile, the ghost
in the frame,

for I cannot help but stare
back and up
at you.

Small breeze
through shirt, one button
too many
undone,

sliver of skin
controls the tide
in me.

Your fingertips
slow like surgeons
to repair the wound.

Mine on yours
to stop their
sewing.

All fire and impact and
the frivolous nature of siege.
My mind, a battering ram
against the locked gates
the world constructs,
shaking bridge over moat
and stone.

I wail at the oil and pour,
dance flame when
fire meets it,
I shout against solid oak
and convince myself
of cracking board,
of eventual entry.

Stand on the ramparts
and watch the war
against myself,

throw down a rope
and let me
climb.

Broken old book
from half-closed shop,
and I open
to quarter-torn
page.

Eyelash pressed
between pages,
stranger's crumbs
from stranger's
eyes,
and I wonder

which words
brought forth the
weeping.

Spoke in drawl,
thick as the sap
of an ashleaf maple,
yes sirs and no ma'ams,
tiny formalities
from a kindergarten tongue.

They laughed it away,
finger-pointed until it hid
in the dark closet
where other secrets hang,
push each other
to avoid the light
when daring hands come
turning rusted knobs.

Sometimes, when exhaustion comes
and I slow,
like engine coal-starved,
chugging on the Seaboard line,
my grandfather's voice,
my father's too before it faded
into the pine and snowfall of north
and west,
slides beneath that closet door,
that thin beam of light
somewhere inside me,

and fills my mouth
with sugar.

As old as light,
this, beginning made and
lasting. Some shine takes
eternities to reach us,
our eyes stay pinpricks
until one day
we're all pupil and awe
and silent maybe
for the first time.

As old as light,
started where it all did,
first moment of noiseless
implosion,

did you know light
ripples across
like water,
did you know it
hits us in
waves?

As old
as light.

One chord
composition,

single note
held
for what must seem like
hours.

Beautiful

as I want
the same.

Put me
small as sunflower seed
in the
hollow
of your throat

where shower
water
sits.

Turn me
to the morning
light.

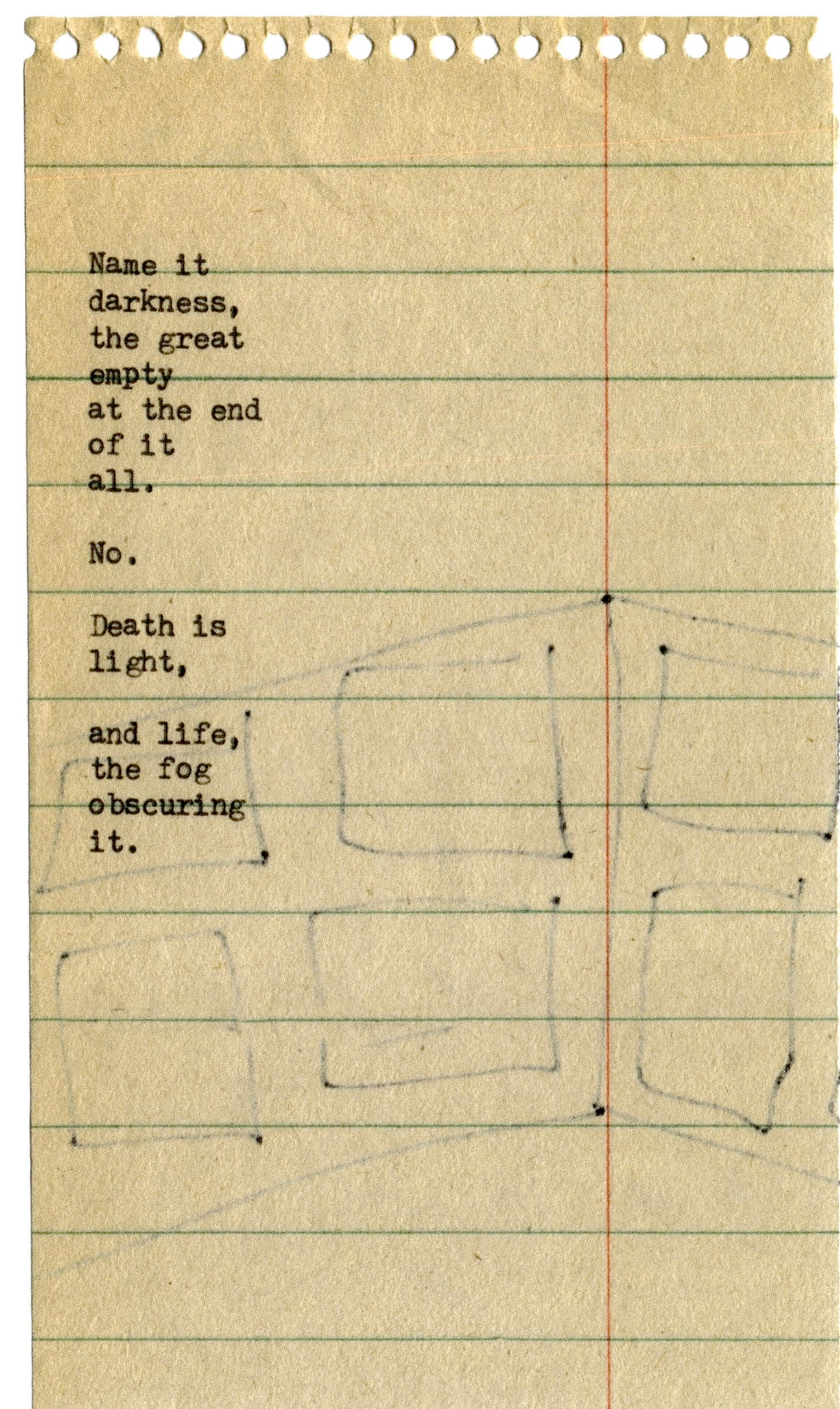

Name it
darkness,
the great
empty
at the end
of it
all.

No.

Death is
light,

and life,
the fog
obscuring
it.

Born with an anchor
made of cork
and I blame it
for my
drifting.

I swear to
you
I am trying so
hard to

stay.

My wife
washing dishes on a night my hands
were on her skin,
I read aloud of Jim Harrison's final words,
the last two penned before he slowed,
then stopped, then returned as new wolf,
or old bird, a stem of wheatgrass rising
through a half-melted snowbank on the
very edge of Yellowstone:

God's body

no punctuation, not a half hint
of a comma or period, pen miles
from even considering it.

The wind picks up and carries
woodsmoke across the valley,
through the long grass poking
through a now-dirty snow.

I wonder what words I will write,
the last before going off
into that unknown night.

There is a pause at the end
of all we know,
all we've named and catalogued,
we know this from a ship sent
on a voyage unreturnable,
asked to sail forever, to call home
from time to time.

Just beyond the fraying threads
of the sun's twirling skirt, wind cast out
like ballerina silk, there is
stillness and windless silence,
a stagnation layer
between this place and
the wild black
beyond.

Speak of evil,
that which we do
to one another,
the snuffing of light,
and say god does not exist.

Speak of beauty,
that which shines
beyond what is solely
necessary,
to the condition of life,
and say that something must.

Call what is beyond us
what you wish,
what I know of faith
is small, and grows
greyer by the
month.

I had no fear of death
before you.

There is death in the things we
will never do again, and we
forget to remember this.

First fingers, electric at the knuckles,
defibrillation in the darkness
at the sliding against another's,
quiet save the breath quickened,
eyes forward as though seeing
would snap the spell.

Not first lips, not again, not
first fevered hands crawling up
a spine in the haze of mouths
and gasps and heads that fall back
and closed eyes and the names
of god called out, not again,
not like that not again.

We remember to forget this.

It's nearly moonlit,
nearly silver
and nothing more.

I've seen the darkness
find light,
watched as
winter
found its way
above your
shoulders.

I'll stare like a
telescope man
with hands fumbling
for the focus.

Sprouting silver from a chin
slowly then swiftly
more like my father's face
every day I wake.

She of crown white
since the start,
a grace I never knew
I could know.

In my mirror I see
aging,
but with each new
strand of
sterling,
somehow
she seems more
alive.

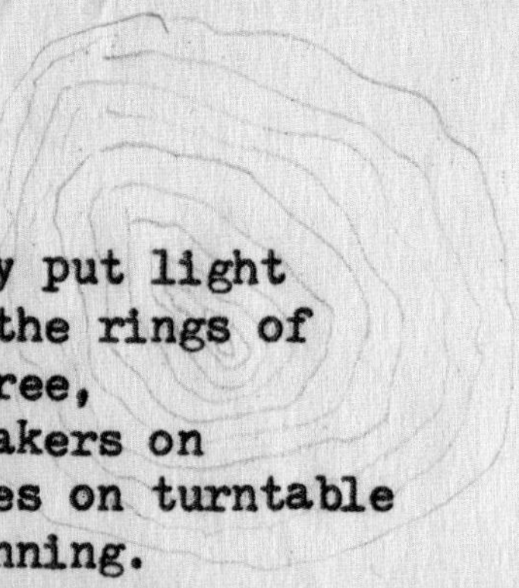

They put light
on the rings of
a tree,
speakers on
wires on turntable
spinning.
Made music
of the years it
grew,
and I wonder if we
were cut the
same, what song
our old bones
would sing.

And with
that

let the great fear
pass.

The end of was,
the start of
is,
we cannot go back
from here.

On the foundation
still smoking
and half alive
with crackling ash
warmth

we must build something
new.

Keep waiting for it to turn around,
life,
for it to show its face
to us, staring at the back
of it all these years,
keep waiting for it to spin on
a heel and meet my eyes.

Waiting for an answer,
for that cavern-dark mouth
to open and
explain.

Waiting to know its voice,
life,
waiting to stare it down
before it walks away
again.

Born of forward feet, of blood
like river down mountain,
forward it thumped like drum
in chest, forward
whispered out in the same language
of wind gust in treetop.

I was a homeless thing,
peripatetic and wandering,
blamed it on the roots of
a family tree, blamed it on
that blood. Forward,
whispered ancestor and
ghost, words for slowing
left untranslated,
curse of a sound left
unmuttered.

Stillness has a sound
and I know this now,
redwood in calm
and all you hear is
its growing. Stay,
you whispered
in the voice of trunk
creaking to quiet,
Stay.

Forward said you
in sigh and softness,
it is only home
if you can bring it
with you.

It will be explosion
and flash
when I go, I know this
because some hold darkness
and transform it
to coruscation,
to glimmer.

I, like tree to our
exhalations,
take your shadow
and absorb,
I give it back like
oxygen,
and ask for you
to come closer
and hold me
as I

disintegrate
into light.

Only time will
show us, decide if
this poison will kill us
or leave us
slowly,
crawling from our blood
like insect from
light.

Even if we
heal,
we'll never be the same.
Some scars
cannot be apologized
away.

We loved like a healing,
like a tangling
of bone and sinew
after break and
wound,

like tender skin
weaving back
together

like marrow

softer
to be

stronger.

Do you know me, after all this time, all
these words? Understand what makes me
tick, what spins the hour hand of this clockwork
brain? I'm 10,000 things— half scare me, half
confuse. I'm a train wreck mind, the giant crunching
jaws that turn cars to scrap, I'm the scrap and the
magnet that it clings to.
I hold my own feet, bare, with warm hands,
soothe myself with the chill and contrast.
I play with my ears, always have, from
when folks swore it'd stick them out
permanent and over-proud. Twirl my hair, too,
but not to the point of bald spot or worry.
I carry mints, not for fresh breath, but breath
at all, same goes for the antihistamines
in the coin pocket, two there, one in the back
as I am terrified of this throat swelling
again.

I am the desperate need of noise-cancelling headphones,
but I'm the guilt and reluctance to use them,
I'm the rub-some-dirt-on-it mentality
to the wounds I endure. I am two million
radios on two million stations and not a single one
has a volume knob. I write to feel sane,
though it only lasts until the final period.
Sisyphus, I call out to the mirrors I avoid,
how heavy is your stone? I am the skin that hurts
when touched gently by all but one,
the fire in the fingers of those who brush
against me. I am dichotomy as sometimes I just need
to be held on to, like the world is spinning and I
cannot get a grip on the floor beneath me.

Parties dismantle me, cannot be a wallflower
as sometimes I'm allergic to the flowers
on the wall. I am incapable of small talk, I
tell truths and don't know if they are too much,
too honest, if they sting when they land. Three
hundred times a minute I remind myself to look
into your eyes. Sometimes, without a moment
of warning, I must go or I am certain I will explode
and the shrapnel of me will discolor their finest
clothes.

I'm the Irish goodbye,
knowing that sooner or later,
I'll see you again.

More struggle than
solace
to get to this
me,
so much more
loss
than gain.

I define myself
by arriving
at all.

Student of a loneliness
few know,
whispered
through whispering teeth
to my shadow, black on
black wall,
sang to it the song
of emptiness.

Called it by
another name,
though it would not
hold my
hand.

What are we
when nothing to no one,
one voice,
calling out in the darkness,
pretending to be
two.

Here the knot tied
to one end of night,
in my fingers
the other,
man of knots, I
double them for strength,

here, tied to the darkness
I ask you to

p
u
l
l

until morning
delays,
until moonglow
lingers

and we do not speak
of day.

Steer clear,

I'm half ghost
half man,

half noise and
half a
silence

that will
haunt you.

Decades spent
chasing it,
borrowing it,
capturing,
stealing for a moment
or two.
Many forms and
many shapes,
many days followed
by many different
moons.

Now I see,
know and understand,

my favorite light
is the
dark.

I have loved you in colors
and I will love you in them all.
Held you in lavender light,
soft bruise of morning
or the healing that comes
just before tangerine spills
and spoils
the earliest moments of arctic,
just before the cobalt,
then denim to slate.

Kissed the pale of you, haven't I?
The alabaster of you before the shower
but after the sheets, charcoal
like storm cloud, put hand to
back when hot water turns
warm porcelain all that once
turned ivory from moonlight.

You of emerald, of cadmium
green like new fern or spring grass
fed on by sheep of pearl
and obsidian, watched you walk
across russet and cider,
over stones painted in iron
and anchor, some pewter,
some mink.

Loved in color, always this,
a slow reduction to only a few,
the sunlit lagoon of your eyes,
the copper mustard dandelion
sunflower that floats
on the surface
of those waters.

If minds had racks, tall as trees
stacks and stacks,
and thoughts were books,
would you understand?
I am lost,
last seen in non-fiction,
or perhaps mysteries,
fumbling out for poetry,
but stuck and cross-legged
in maps and atlases
of the world.
If you shouted down
the corridors, heard
echo as paper bound
does not insulate, would
you then see what it feels like
in here?

Sit and I'll build you a chair
before you hit the ground,
a lamp on a desk
and an oath of silence
that I don't know how
to break.

Away now
you beautiful evil,
off and stay
gone.

Keep closed
the box,
and let us rewind
to the before,

when they knew
you'd come
and feared you
still.

We are halfway
to ruin,
too distracted
to even
notice.

A boy of the birds
was I,
palm open with seed
and hope,
tenderness that called them
in.

Never fit, when fitting
began, floated like bubble
unpoppable and light,
bounced where others burst,
showed you yourself
if you got close enough,
distorted but
beautiful.

Boy of the birds,
I was,
eyes to the dance
of murmuration
on spring sky,
the quiet patience
that told me
they'd always come back
home.

Here and here and all
of the wheres

there isn't
an inch untouched,

a fraction of this
flesh

that doesn't miss
you.

You've not enough
fingers to point

to every spot
that aches.

I am lucky as peach pie
under ice cream dripping
on some sweltering
summer day

she is the cobbler, the crust,
the plate and fork,
she is the spoon,
the bowl, the drip of joy,
the firework exploding
in early July sky.

She she she the whistle the pop

the carnation of color in
a field of night,

she she she a thousand times she,
the celebration

of my melting.

Tell me
what you're afraid
to say you
like,

tell me what you're
ashamed
you
desire.

I'll meet you
just beyond
that border wall.

I will join you
and bring blush
to those
cheeks.

I'll take tonight, should it be all and only,
should I fade into chalk dust
and ghost letters after erasing,
should I catch fire
when sunrise peeks over ocean still
and soft as ribbon,
should I forget the waking
that follows the trusting
of shutting these eyes in
the darkness of the room
we share.

Tonight, and call it satisfactory,
call myself content
that I'll never know what comes
after these hours,
these of twisted limbs and
breath passed back and forth,
heavy with sigh and
sweetness.

Tonight, and ask your silent hand
to squeeze it, if it
agrees.

All the miles
on these aching feet,
the hours of layover
blending into
another.

All I've seen
hidden amongst the rubble
of everything
from the broken bits of
everywhere

taught me this
(chiefly, above all the millions of
minor others):

Love,
truest and most fundamental,
lasting and stronger
than blood,

is tenderness
and almost nothing
else.

A man offers options
for dessert
to his wife, struggling
to remember his
name.

Talk to me of light,
the speed at which
a star finds my eyes,
tell me that it's long
since dead,
but make it sound
hopeful.

Some are terrified
of being here
when it's all gone black,
time catches up
and there's no more
glow to reach
us.

But I know darkness
as a limbed thing,

I have felt it hold me.

This heart of mine,
made of monks three:

one to know, faith-drenched
with forward eyes, one to
convince the other two
to brave the sea,

to sail to barren rock,
empty but for gannets, for
terns, gulls, and cormorants,

stabbing sky from the ocean
that churns,

and declare it home.

Hundreds aimed at sunset
over its peak and fell
to knees

for a sermon they could not see,
for words they could not
hear.

If you want more words
it is more you shall have.
I will stare into the creek
until the bed runs dry.

Always, they come,
boats after boats all folded
by hand.

Terror comes in not knowing
if the hands were my own.

Words on words on words,
these are yours
even when rubbish,
even when misspelled or
garbage or worth half of
nothing.

Still then.
Still.

I will be forgotten,
sand in water drug
back to sea, I will
dissolve and hope one
day for distillation,
for some purity of
self, of soul.

We come to terms with
our impermanence,
transients on old rail line,
rattling doors and eyelids
slowly shut. Lie,
we do,
and say we're ok
with not being remembered.

For one brief evanescent
and vanishing breath,
I was here, and I loved
so hard.

Let's stay until we're
accents and
understanding.
I want feet
that know the songs
of the stones they
stand upon,
I want hands dirty
from handshake and
holding,
I want to whisper
of wild things
and know
every sound is heard.

Let's stay
and dissolve into the
soft fabric
our wishes have
woven.

Come to the sleeping place
and call it cathedral

as I worship at the altar
of your paleness.

I speak aloud the gospel
of our heat,

shape your lips into ring
as you call out

the name of some god
over and again

through teeth on blanket
or the corners

of my shoulders, slowly
trembling.

To the all of you
who do not know me,
though say you
may:

mountains you have missed,
seas and islands green,
mist and light
thick enough to slice

some shining landscape
in me, harbor
from the storms that come
and come again
though you nail wood to
windows to brace
against.

This is in me,
half day's journey
beyond the shoreline
of my skin,

just beyond the hurricane
that darkens my
horizon.

Follow the
breadcrumbs

the pants
and shirt sock and
what was
under
thrown over
and aside

if we get lost,
stuck in
sheets

these will lead us
back

or show them the way
back to
us.

Forgetful lot,
we,
misplace the understanding
that all was green
once,
and all will be green
again.

Green will come
and green will
stay,
try as we might,
try as we
may,
we too will be

green again,

only not in
envy,
but in

decay.

Old photograph
of old love
hidden
from intolerance
and hate.

We look back
and forget
that they too
loved in
color.

Thin is the thread
that holds me
to this
society,
spiderweb delicate
and I hope
just as
strong.

I see it when
the light
shifts,
watch it throw
rainbow
as ~~though~~ though prismatic.

You
are the thread,
the arachnid silk
keeping me
here,

go
and I will
fall.

Sit you, you there across
a room, sit and
leak out into this
universe
all that grace.

I'll stay, me, clumsy
and fumbling,
perhaps
some will spill,

waft over
and fall asleep on
these

tired shoulders.

Add the spaces
for the
breaths
as I
    am without them

when I

  spill.

Punctuation
like a
  lifeline

I call each
comma

salvation.

I'll lift from this.

I'll rise up,
fog
off sea water
in the half glow
of dawn,

roll to a shore
after a
time

and seek out
sunrise.

You will know me
by the light
I hold.

Never back, not the
rewind to when hand
was small to mine
large, when I
led you down cobbled street,
past gravestone and
mustachioed men in
haunted light,
not back to small
and atop stone
before promises were
spoken
into a wall of rainfall
and the
passing of that
storm.

Forward, with the
tears of this
truth.

Thankful I was born the way I was, raised by family
tiptoe-reaching for middle-class. I am now what I
was then, and I am proud of what I was.

I was a well-worn jacket that knew my big sisters' arms
before mine, then passed down and learned the skin
of my little sister after me.
I was the fast-food dinner once a month, the happy meal
toy while my parents shared a sandwich.
I was the puppet show of sock and imagination,
the wonder in a wander through Cone Park, the stillness
of the Blue Ridge.
I was chicken pox twice in a year, I was a spider bite
above my eye. I was the homemade costume, Karate Kid
on a budget.
I was the lightning bugs I chased, I was the poison ivy itch,
I was the fireworks on the fourth of July,
hands-in-head and ball cap on my stomach, I was the outfield grass
and the youth small replica uniform,
I was the 33 my dad wore, I was the 6 7/8 size hat that still
didn't quite fit.

I was the VW van and the thousands of miles across the
backroads of America, I was the soda cans cooling
in forest stream, I was the hands holding the ladder
while my father painted some Southern house. I was the
arrowhead in the sand with my hand in my grandfather's.
I was the wood chopped, the axe that split, I was
the dirty hands reaching for hot dog cooked
over campfire, I was the innocence before it all.

I was the train whistle in the cicada song of
some sweltering night, the doodlebug fishing in the dirt
below the azaleas, I was the pancake breakfast, I was the
shell hunt at low tide.

I was the lesson that magic grows wild, even where money doesn't.

A lift and a
peek
window to skin
porthole to
a bit of
you
that disrupts
the bloodflow
in me

that rearranges its
gravity.

Lather me in
your hands.

I will go
where the soap
will go.

Smooth like
silk
to
all the places
you want me
to
reach.

I want to peel you
off of me
like t-shirt after
water dip,
like rind
from orange,
burst like
tiny volcanos
citrus spray
into morning
light,

like second skin
left by snake
transformed
on some sizzling
desert
floor.

Ink on canvas
on page
on skin,
we become
art
with the love
we let
in.

Robert A. McKinnon
PAE
3.00

Lit by death we are,
illuminated
by the silent passing
of six billion stars.
The cemetery above us,
the glistening graveyard filled
with tombstones of light.

Sadness has a scent
only some can smell it.
Rain on firework smoke,
sparkler in a snowstorm.

Maybe when we go,
we still shine on those
left behind,
maybe it's years of
illumination,
maybe they lift their
eyes to us,
maybe for a moment,
they too
catch the aroma
on the breeze.

If the burden of me
is too much to bear,

set me down
and I will kiss
your blameless lips
goodbye.

Do not suffer
to love
me.

Let's learn the word for light
in every language so when
we chase what we chase
and when we go
where we go
we will know
what to
call
it.

I got a thing
for the way people
look
when they're lost
in a book,
breath like a forgotten
promise,
heart that beats
outside a
chest.

Frenzy locked in
stillness.

You're the handcuff
the radiator, the bolt
to the floor,
you're the concrete
the boots
the bottom of the
sea.

You're the tether
the clasp
the zip tie
and the wrist,

you're the anchor
the rope
the refusal to drop
all you used to
be.

You're the knife
the flame
the saw blade
glistening,
you're the bolt cutters
the hands that
hold them.

A thousand things
we call it,

decorate it with
a thousand
words,

what it settles on,
this dust of
our hearts
wandering,

we're all in search
of home.

-Tyler Knott Gregson-

More trees than stars,
factor of 8,
3 trillion rooted,
spinning
as we
spin,

still we stare
up

searching
for somewhere else
to call

home.

You came in
like breeze through
open window,
like stream
to stormy sea,
like lover
after months
of anticipation and
ache.

Frayed
though you may
feel,

forget not
that it is here,
at the severing
of our
ropes,

softness
is born.

149 Union Avenue
Memphis, Tennessee 38103

I bite my lip,
knuckle,
the side of your
leg
beside my mouth when
yes
and
more
and not quite
enough breath
to hold
it.

In place of words
give me lips,
in lieu of
kisses

give me
promises.

To love is to lose,
but it is the aftermath of loss
that pulls the net
from below our tightrope feet.
We are such heights
without the grace of safety,
we are the aching understanding
that the further we feel
the more it will hurt.

One foot, two,
left foot over right,
don't look down but
forward. Arms wide
to hold more than balance,
but the world as it
spins.

Look at me
from where you are,
look at my stillness despite
the winds.

I would fly if I fell,
and I know you always loved
a winged thing.

All this time
fighting
to prove you're
enough,

blind to already
being
brilliantly
beyond it.

Watch
the horizon line

hopeful eyes
fuzzy with tears

call out to me
with hello voice

just loud enough
for me to hear.

We invent time
with the stories
we tell,
we set the pace
with how we
live.

Quickly it passes
when we
love,
slowly it drags
when we
search for
it.

You're the pillow
against the
window pane,
you're the breeze
that summer gave,
you're the long
drive,
you're the
feet
on the dash,
you're the road,
god dammit you're
the road.

Half an inch between
my hand
and your hand
and I learned more
of intimacy
than in two and a half
dozen years
before.

One touch and
I knew.

To think I thought things over,
to think I thought I knew
the colors of a life,
the way light could come
and throw hope
like lilies
into the valley of our days.

Took a lifetime of wrong
to find one right,
took digging up the weeds
in the garden of us
to understand what it is
to bloom.

Some are built of peace
and some of ache,
some built on the sorrow
that distance plants, on the
weight of waiting.
We are the blossom
after years of drought,

we are the lily,
we are the valley,
we are the light pouring
into every shadowed place.

Bravery is catching,
courage
contagious,

be what you're made
to be,

watch
as all those that
witness it

find it possible
to do the
same.

Woke beside
you, unveiled,
raw,
and nearer
to understanding
what it is they
speak about
when they speak
of god.

I don't want to
know
this world
without you in
it.

I read to you
in morning
voice,

I watch you
towel-dry yourself
fresh
from the
bath.

Maybe they fit,
take the shape to match it,
lay flat against
the raised bits before
the nerves die
and color no longer
finds it.

Words for wounds
unseen
but singing out,

sentences like
stitches

to the slices
you bear.

I will write until
you call yourself
healed.

Give me the glass
that splits that light,
scatters it,
fragmentations
of all that rests
behind it,

I want you
in ten thousand
pieces

wet
from shower steam

some
kaleidoscope

of skin and
sighs.

I think I used to be more joyful,
6-year-old wonder that never quite faded,
pirate hat scavenger hunt of a thing, stuffed
into the seams I can't stop scratching at now.
I think I held it longer, filled up with wide-eyed
optimism and passion like a fever, I think
I used to be more joyful.

Time is a thief, pickpocket on some busy street,
you never feel the hand, never feel
the watch slide off your wrist.
You aim someplace, tourist in tourist shoes,
only to arrive empty and broke, fumbling
for a wallet you swore you still felt
in your back left pocket, check the hour
on a watch already halfway to the pawn shop.
I tell myself it was stolen, call myself victim
for losing the capacity for happiness,
the forfeiture of some reckless bliss,
but this is a lie I tell to sleep sounder,
this is a lie I tell for I think I used to be
more joyful, and I don't want to carry the blame
for letting it float away.
Time is a thief, this is a truth, but some things
we give away.

I am tired of cynicism masquerading as realism,
tired of blaming the world and its catastrophic
implosion for the colors I paint my days in,
for the choices I make without understanding
why. I think I used to be more joyful,
and I think it's time I was again. In some dusty
corner of my mind, there's a costumed kid
who still believes absolutely anything
is possible.

You warm your hands
under water
you open your
mouth
when there's too much
good
to fit

you melt the ice
in me, you

make it alright
to be
just a bit
too much,
just a step
too far.

We'll like the taste of it
in our mouths
when the time comes,
when we say it.
Roll it around awhile,
hold it in our
cheeks,
see whose lasts longest.

After ten thousand
thousand
hellos, I think we
finally understand,

the sweetest goodbyes
are
earned.

Swallower of
sorrow,
I wish I was, bigger
mouth, stomach
to hold it.
I'd bite into what
hurt you
and chew until
it was
nothing at
all.

This unruly head
of electrified hair,
this mop of
honeyed wheat
reaching for the
sky,

perhaps I'm tugged at
by the moon,
perhaps like Nin

the stars are pulling me
away.

I think myself a man
of trembling heart.

I know it shakes
but still

thumps on.

Still it
thunders.

Tyler Knott Gregson is the celebrated author of six books, including the national bestseller *Chasers of the Light*. His work has touched readers around the world, with nearly 300,000 copies sold and translations into seven languages. Gregson's poetry has been featured in *The New York Times, The Wall Street Journal, NPR*, and more, and he has collaborated with brands like Nordstrom, Spotify, and Ralph Lauren. Following his adult Autism diagnosis, Gregson's work has taken on new depth, exploring themes of identity and acceptance. He lives in Montana with his wife, Sarah Linden Gregson, and their work continues to inspire a global community of readers.